Billie
the Baby Goat
Fairy

To Nancy, Nell, and Peggy

Special thanks to Rachel Elliot

ISBN 978-1-338-20700-2

10 9 8 7 6 5 4 3 2 1   18 19 20 21 22

Printed in the U.S.A.   40
First printing 2018

Billie
the Baby Goat Fairy

by Daisy Meadows

SCHOLASTIC INC.

The Fairyland Palace

Farmhouse

Pond

Fluttering Fairyland Farm

Greenfields Farm

Greenfields House

Barn

Pond

I want a farm that's just for me,
With animals I won't set free.
It's far too slow to find each one.
Let fairy magic get this done!

With magic from the fairy farm,
I'll grant my wish—to their alarm!
And if I spoil the humans' fun,
Then Jack Frost really will have won!

Contents

A Big Day and a Big Problem

The sun was shining brightly on Greenfields Farm, and the fresh early-morning breeze made it the perfect spring day. Butterflies and bees were already busy around the flowers and bushes. Rachel Walker and her best friend, Kirsty Tate, were walking away from the farmhouse, feeling a very special kind of excitement.

"The big day has finally arrived," said Kirsty, pausing to take a long, deep breath of fresh country air. "I can't wait for the grand opening to start!"

The girls—together with Kirsty's parents—had been staying at the farm during spring break to help the Tates' friends Harriet and Niall Hawkins get the farm ready to welcome visitors.

"I want to be sure that everything is perfect," said Rachel.

The girls had been given the very special job of looking after the baby farm animals. They had loved every minute of it, and this morning they had woken up extra early so that they could check on all the baby animals before the grand opening.

"Let's visit the ducklings first," said Kirsty.

They walked past the barn and along the winding path that led to the duck pond. As soon as they had walked between the trees, they saw the glittering water of the pond, with its tall cattails and its happy ducks. Lots of little ducklings were quacking as they splashed around.

"They all look fine," said Rachel. "Shall we check the lambs next? I love the way they bounce around when they see us. It's as if they've got springs in their hooves."

In the sheep pasture, the lambs bounced just as lambs should, and Rachel and Kirsty gave them some food and patted their fluffy white wool. Their eager baaing made the girls smile.

"Foals next," said Kirsty. "I wonder if

they will still be clean after the bath we gave them yesterday?"

"No way," said Rachel, laughing. "You know how much they love rolling in all those muddy puddles."

Sure enough, when they arrived at the stables, they found all the foals coated in mud, neighing happily as they rolled and splashed.

"I'm so glad they're all OK," said Kirsty. "Thank goodness Jack Frost and his pesky goblins haven't caused any more trouble."

"At least not yet," said Rachel.

On their first day at Greenfields Farm, Kirsty and Rachel had met the Farm Animal Fairies and visited the Fluttering Fairyland Farm, a magical farm hovering in midair among the puffy white clouds. The Farm Animal Fairies—Debbie the Duckling Fairy, Elodie the Lamb Fairy, Penelope the Foal Fairy, and Billie the Baby Goat Fairy—showed the girls their magical baby farm animals, who lived at the farm.

But while the girls were visiting the rest of the animals with Francis the Fairyland farmer, Jack Frost stole the magical farm animals, Splashy the duckling, Fluffy the lamb, Frisky the foal, and Chompy the baby goat.

"I keep thinking about poor Snowdrop and the mother snow goose," said Kirsty. "I hope they're getting a bit more love and attention from Jack Frost now."

Jack Frost had taken the farm animals because he wanted his own private petting zoo at his Ice Castle. The snow goose and her baby, Snowdrop, were Jack Frost's pets, and they loved him to pieces. But Jack had been so busy chasing after the magical baby farm animals that he had been neglecting the snow geese.

"Me, too," said Rachel. "But most of all, I'm thinking about Billie the Baby Goat Fairy. The fairies need *all* the magical baby farm animals to be safe, or they won't be able to look after baby farm animals everywhere. As long as Chompy is missing, the fairies can't look after the animals."

Over their last few days at Greenfields Farm, Rachel and Kirsty had seen baby farm animals doing some very strange things indeed. The ducklings had acted like puppies, the lambs had acted like kittens, and the foals had acted like piglets. So far, the girls had managed to get three of the fairies' magical baby animals back from Jack Frost and his mischievous goblins. But Chompy the baby goat was still missing.

Rachel and Kirsty made their way to the fenced pen where the goats lived. Gilbert, the baby, was always waiting for them at the top of the arched bridge. But today, something was wrong. The bridge was empty.

"Where is he?" asked Kirsty.

They hurried over, and then they saw the little goat. He wasn't prancing around like usual. He was pecking the ground and making a very strange sound.

"It's almost like clucking," said Kirsty.

She and Rachel turned to each other as they realized what had happened.

"Gilbert thinks he's a chicken," said Rachel. "Jack Frost and his naughty goblins are still causing trouble."

"We have to find Chompy," said Kirsty, looking at her watch. "The farm opens in an hour. There's no time to lose!"

Panic in the Henhouse

Just then, Kirsty let out an excited little squeal.

"Rachel, look at that bucket of feed in the goat pen," she said.

It seemed to be an ordinary metal bucket, but Rachel trusted her best friend. She knew of only one thing that could make Kirsty sound so excited in the middle of a crisis. Fairy magic! She stared

at the bucket, and
then she saw a
little flare of
sparkling
light. It grew
brighter, until
the whole bucket
was glowing.
Then a tiny,
glittering fairy
shot out of the
bucket and high into
the air. She
whizzed around
like a firework, and then swooped down
to where the girls were standing.

"Hello, Rachel and Kirsty," she said,
a little out of breath. "It's me, Billie the
Baby Goat Fairy."

Billie was wearing blue overalls with white polka dots and a T-shirt with ruffled, flowy sleeves. Her eyes twinkled behind her glasses.

"Hello, Billie," said Rachel. "We're really glad to see you. Look at poor Gilbert—he thinks he's a chicken."

Billie fluttered down and perched on the top of the wooden fence. As soon as she saw Gilbert pecking the ground, she folded her arms and shook her head.

"I *must* get Chompy back home," she said. "I can't help any baby goats until we've found him. I came to tell you that one of the goblins has brought Chompy here to the farm. Will you help me search for him?"

"We're always glad to help our fairy friends," said Kirsty at once. "Where shall we look first?"

"It'll be easier to search the farm if we can fly over it and search for Chompy from above," said Rachel.

"Good thinking," said Billie, snapping her fingers. "No sooner said than done."

The girls ducked down behind the gate of the pen. They couldn't see anyone watching, but they didn't want to take any risks. Nobody else could find out about the fairies.

Billie waved her wand, and a flurry of springtime flowers rose up and swirled around the girls, hiding them from view. Surrounded by the magical blooms, Rachel and Kirsty felt themselves shrinking to fairy size. Their hair was sprinkled with petals as their fairy wings grew. Then the flowers fell to the ground and the three fairies flew upward together. From the air, they could see the whole farmyard laid out like a map.

"There are the pigs, the sheep, and
the horses," said Kirsty as they flew over
Greenfields Farm.

"No sign of the goblin or Chompy,"
said Kirsty. "There's Blossom the cow
beside the barn—we should check
inside."

They swooped into the barn, but it was
empty. Blossom let out a worried moo,
and the fairies paused to pat her.

"Don't worry,
Blossom,"
Rachel
whispered in
her ear. "We're
trying to help
the farm."

Blossom nodded
her head in the direction of the chicken
coop behind the farmhouse. When the
fairies flew closer, they heard squawking,
flapping, and alarmed clucking.

"Something is scaring the chickens,"
said Kirsty.

They zoomed across to the chicken
coop and landed beside the ramp that
led into the henhouse. A baby goat was
standing in the entrance, and the golden
glow of his coat told them who he was.

"Chompy!" said Billie.

Suddenly, Chompy started moving down the ramp, and the fairies saw that a goblin was trying to grab him. Chompy tried to leave the henhouse, but the goblin threw his arms around the baby goat's neck.

"Stop clucking," the goblin wailed. "I want to cuddle with you!"

But Chompy butted him and disappeared. The squawking of the hens grew louder.

"Why is Chompy playing around the henhouse?" Rachel asked.

"Maybe he wants to sit on a nest like the hens," said Kirsty. "After all, he is acting like a chicken."

Suddenly, an idea popped into Rachel's head.

"That's exactly what we need," she said. "A nest! Billie, can you make one big enough for Chompy to sit on?"

Billie waved her wand and a large nest appeared on the ground outside the henhouse.

"It's the perfect size for Chompy," said Rachel in delight. "Chompy, over here!"

Chompy scampered over and sat down on the big nest, clucking happily.

"Chompy," said Billie, fluttering toward him. He looked up at her and gave a confused little frown.

Rachel and Kirsty held hands and smiled. Any moment now, Chompy would be back to his normal self. But suddenly, there was a loud crack, and a bolt of icy blue magic zigzagged through the sky. And then Jack Frost was standing in front of the nest.

Jack Frost's Shadows

Jack Frost dove for Chompy, but the magical baby goat lunged out of the nest and ran, squawking like a frightened chicken.

"Come back!" Jack Frost roared.

He raced after Chompy, and the fairies chased them both as fast as they could.

Rachel glanced back over her shoulder and saw a flurry of feathers as the goblin sat down among the chickens, wailing. Rachel almost felt sorry for him. Then she looked ahead again and saw Jack Frost charging after Chompy, yelling.

"They're going to cause chaos," Rachel said with a groan.

Harriet and Niall had spent the day before putting up signs and banners for the visitors. There were signs to direct people to the pigs, the sheep, the horses, and the goats, as well as the barn and the welcome center. There were banners advertising tractor rides, donkey rides, bottle-feeding the baby farm animals, pig races, and baby-animal cuddles. Hay bales had been placed here and there for visitors to sit on.

But as Chompy hurtled across the farm, he wasn't looking where he was going. All

he cared about was getting away from
Jack Frost. He bumped into the signs and
knocked them down. He ran straight at
the banners with his head down, ripping
them and scattering them across the
farm. Jack Frost stampeded after him,
flinging hay bales out of his way to the
left and right.

The fairies fluttered overhead, feeling helpless. There was nothing they could do to stop the rampage.

"He's ruining everything," said Kirsty. "All the hard work we've been doing will be undone. If the visitors see the farm looking like this, they will never come back. We have to stop Jack Frost and save Chompy."

"I don't understand why Jack Frost is still so set on stealing baby animals for his petting zoo," said Kirsty. "He's got his own baby goose, Snowdrop, back at his Ice Castle—and his other snow goose, too. They love him. Why is he so greedy for more?"

"He is never happy with the things he has," said Rachel. "Jack Frost always wants what other people have."

Just then, something caught her eye and she looked away from the chase. Two white shapes were following Jack Frost like shadows as he weaved across the farm.

"It's Snowdrop and her mother," said Kirsty. "They must have followed Jack Frost all the way from the Ice Castle."

"They really love Jack Frost," said Billie.

"They don't stop caring about him just because he's trying to find other animals."

"I've got an idea," said Kirsty. "We need to show Jack Frost what he's missing— and the snow geese can help us."

The three fairies hovered close together and Kirsty whispered her plan. Feeling hopeful, they all flew down to land in a field behind the barn. The snow geese were waddling toward them, a long way behind Jack Frost and Chompy. Billie

waved her wand, and a bowl of crisp
green lettuce appeared beside the snow
geese. They noticed it, and hurried over
to nibble on the lettuce.

The fairies fluttered down beside them
and spoke in soft voices.

"We want to talk to Jack Frost," said
Kirsty. "Will you help us?"

The snow geese honked and nodded.

Gently, the fairies climbed onto the mother snow goose's back, scooping Snowdrop up with them.

"We'll follow Chompy and Jack Frost together," said Kirsty. "And when we reach them, we'll find a way to make Jack Frost see what wonderful pets he already has."

Ice-Cold Heart

They soared into the sky and zoomed over the farm. It was delightful to be surrounded by the soft, white feathers of the snow geese.

"It's like sitting inside a cloud," Rachel said with excitement.

The farm was a terrible mess, but the fairies were looking for just one thing—a little baby goat. At last they spotted him, and the snow goose changed direction. Chompy was in the goat pen, standing in the middle of the arched bridge. Jack Frost had his arms around the little goat and was cuddling him tightly and cackling with laughter.

"Stop struggling," Jack Frost was saying. "You're *my* pet now. You're going

to live in a lovely icy home. You'll like it.
Yes, you will."

Chompy wasn't listening. He was
wiggling, squawking, and flapping his
legs as if they were wings. But Jack Frost
kept holding on, stopping him from
getting away.

The snow goose let out a sad little
honk and fluttered downward, perching
on the railing of the bridge. The fairies
fluttered down to stand beside her, and
Jack Frost stared at them all in surprise.

"What are you doing here?" he
asked the snow goose. "And why are
you hanging around with those pesky
fairies?"

"They're allowed to have friends," said
Billie.

"Oh, no, they're not," Jack Frost

snapped. "They've got *me*. They don't need anyone else."

"Of course they are allowed to have other friends," said Billie. "And so is Chompy. He belongs at Fluttering Fairyland Farm with the other magical baby animals."

"You're not going to get him back, ever," said Jack Frost. "He belongs with me now."

He cuddled Chompy even more tightly. Chompy gave a grumpy squawk.

"He doesn't belong with you," Rachel said. "He belongs with Billie. He's not his true self without her."

"I'm taking Chompy to my petting zoo at the Ice Castle," Jack Frost shouted. "That's where the snow geese should be, too. And once we're all there, no silly fairies are going to stop us."

The mother snow goose gave another miserable little honk, and Rachel looked into Jack Frost's cold eyes.

"Perhaps the snow geese came to find you here because they've been missing you," said Rachel.

Kirsty saw the sad look on Snowdrop's face and nodded.

"Maybe they think that you don't love them anymore," she said. "You've been so busy trying to get animals for your petting zoo that you've stopped thinking about the snow geese."

Chompy struggled again, dragging Jack Frost across the bridge.

"He doesn't *want* to be your pet," Kirsty called out. "But there are two animals here who *do* want to be with you."

Jack Frost stared at her, still clasping Chompy as tightly as he could. The mother snow goose nodded her long neck in agreement, and Snowdrop fluttered up to sit on Jack's shoulder.

"The baby farm animals don't want to be part of your petting zoo," Rachel

said. "But the snow geese truly love
you."

The other fairies held their breaths as
they watched. Could the geese touch the
Ice Lord's cold heart?

Jack Frost's Perfect Pets

Jack Frost looked at the mother snow goose, who tilted her head to one side. Snowdrop nuzzled his cheek with soft, white feathers. Chompy was still pulling away from him, but his snow geese were longing to be with him.

Very slowly, Jack Frost loosened his long, bony fingers from Chompy's wiry

hair. He took his arms away from
Chompy's neck. The little goat hurried
away, and Billie
fluttered over to
him. As soon
as she touched
him, he shrank
to fairy size
and bleated
happily.

"No more
chicken noises,"
said Rachel,
smiling. "He's
back to his normal self."

"Yes," said Billie. "And it's all thanks to
you, Rachel and Kirsty."

"You're welcome," said Kirsty. "We're
just happy that you have Chompy back."

Jack Frost patted little Snowdrop, who sat on his shoulder, and walked over to pet the snow goose. She lifted her head, and he stroked her gently. As Rachel and Kirsty watched, they saw his chin wobble. He sniffed, and then a tear rolled down his cheek.

"I'm so glad you love me," he said.

"Because I I-I-I . . ."

The fairies stared at the Ice Lord as he stammered.

"He's *really* not used to saying this word," said Kirsty.

Jack took a deep breath.

"I l-l-love you, too," he said.

Rachel and Kirsty shared a smile.

"It's good to hear Jack Frost talking about happy feelings for a change," said Rachel.

"It's a truly happy ending," said Kirsty. "All except for the mess that Chompy and Jack Frost made on the farm. How are we going to explain it?"

"You won't have to," said Billie, tucking Chompy under her arm. "Follow me."

They all fluttered over Greenfields Farm and Billie waved her wand, sprinkling fairy dust across the farm. When it landed, the broken signs were instantly fixed and the torn banners were repaired in a flash. The hay bales rolled back into position and all the stray pieces of straw were swept up.

"Are you going to take Chompy back to Fairyland now?" Rachel asked.

"Yes," said Billie. "Chompy and the rest of the magical baby animals are best looked after by Farmer Francis at

Fluttering Fairyland Farm."

"It's such a lovely place," said Kirsty. "I hope we can see it again some day."

"How about today?" Billie asked with a smile. "Would you like to come for another visit right now?"

"Yes, please!" Rachel and Kirsty said together.

The three fairies flew down to where Jack Frost was still cuddling his snow geese.

"You should come to Fluttering Fairyland Farm, too," Billie said to Jack Frost. "I want to show you what a farm is like when the animals *want* to be there."

Jack Frost nodded, and Billie raised her wand. A sparkling flash of fairy dust whooshed around the little group, surrounding them with bands of light.

They were dazzled by it, and when the light faded, they blinked and gazed around in wonder. They were once more standing on the lush green grass of Fluttering Fairyland Farm. Farmer Francis was in front of them, and he smiled when he saw Jack Frost cuddling the snow geese.

"I see that Billie, Rachel, and Kirsty have shown you that the pets you already have are special," said Francis.

Jack Frost had a real
smile on his face,
and everyone
could see that
for once, he
was feeling
truly happy.

"Your
animals are
nice," Jack Frost
said to Billie. "But my
snow geese are the best."

"That's exactly how you *should* feel
about your own pets," said Billie. "And
I'm glad you like ours, too. But please
don't take them away from us again."

"You can visit the animals at the farm
whenever you want," said Farmer Francis.

"I would like that," said Jack Frost.

"But right now I am going to take my snow geese back home to the Ice Castle."

The mother snow goose snuggled into him and he stroked her feathers. He darted a suspicious look around for a moment, and then lowered his voice.

"I'm so sorry that I wasn't kind enough to you both," he whispered. "I want to make it up to you with lots of love and cuddling."

The snow geese honked happily and Jack Frost looked around again.

"Why is he looking so worried?" asked Kirsty.

"I think he's checking that there are no goblins around," said Rachel, laughing. "He wouldn't want them to hear him being so nice."

Farmer Francis turned to her and smiled.

"You and Kirsty are always welcome visitors, too," he said. "There are four animals here who will always be grateful to you."

He stepped aside, and the girls saw the other three Farm Animal Fairies, together with their magical baby animals. The

fairies flew over to hug Rachel and
Kirsty, and the animals gathered in, too,
all happily back to their normal selves.

"Thank you again, for everything,"
said Billie. "We wouldn't be here without
you."

Rachel and Kirsty gave each of the
magical animals a cuddle. Then, as the
fairies waved good-bye, Billie raised
her wand. In a blink, the girls found
themselves standing beside the goat pen.
They were back on Greenfields Farm.

Open for Visitors

Gilbert was exactly where he belonged—standing by the arched bridge and bleating.

"He's back to normal," said Kirsty.

"And at last, all the baby farm animals are themselves again," said Rachel. "Thank goodness."

They shared a
happy glance as
Harriet appeared
around the side of
the farmhouse. She
waved at them.

"The official
opening is about to
start," she called. "Come
on—you don't want to miss it after all
your hard work."

Rachel and Kirsty raced across the
farm to join her. Niall was waiting for
them at the front of the farmhouse,
together with Kirsty's parents. They all
walked down to the main entrance gate,
sharing a lovely feeling of excitement.

"This is going to be a wonderful day,"
said Rachel happily.

"I hope we've thought of everything," said Harriet.

Niall squeezed her hand and smiled.

"The visitors will love it," said Mrs. Tate in a confident voice. "You have turned Greenfields Farm into the perfect family day out."

There were lots of people at the main gate, and a red ribbon had been hung across the entrance. At the front of the crowd were two girls who looked about the same age as Rachel and Kirsty.

"Those girls are Emily and Isabel," said Niall. "They won our competition to officially open the farm and be the first-ever visitors. Rachel and Kirsty, after the ceremony, will you show them around?"

Rachel and Kirsty nodded at once. They always loved the chance to make new friends.

"Emily and Isabel look really nice," said Kirsty. "I can't wait to show them all the sweet baby animals."

Niall and Harriet greeted the visitors and gave Emily and Isabel a special pair of enormous golden scissors.

"They make me feel as if we've shrunk to fairy size again," Rachel whispered, smiling at her best friend.

Emily used the giant scissors to cut the red ribbon.

"We now declare Greenfields Farm open for visitors," Isabel announced.

The crowd clapped and cheered, and then Harriet brought Emily and Isabel over to meet the girls.

"Rachel and Kirsty will show you around the farm," she said. "I hope you have a wonderful day."

Rachel and Kirsty linked arms with Emily and Isabel, and together they walked up toward the animals.

"What would you like to see first?"

Rachel asked the two girls.

"The lambs," said Emily.

"The ducklings," said Isabel.

The girls laughed, sharing the excitement of their new friends. Soon they were running around the farm together, hurrying from baby animal to baby animal, until Emily and Isabel had seen almost every single one.

"Just Gilbert left to visit," said Kirsty at last. "And we know where he'll be."

Sure enough, when they reached the goat pen, Gilbert was standing on the arched bridge.

When he saw Rachel and Kirsty, he let out a happy bleat and clomped down from the bridge. There was a big crowd of people watching him, and they cheered and smiled when they saw how much Gilbert loved his visitors. Laughing, the girls petted him, but Emily and Isabel hung back.

"Don't be afraid," said Rachel, looking up at them. "He's really sweet. He might try to nibble your clothes, but he won't hurt you."

Emily and Isabel stepped closer. At first they were nervous, but after a few moments they realized how gentle the baby goat was. Soon all four girls were petting Gilbert, and he was delighted.

"He's gorgeous," said Emily.

Kirsty waved to her parents in the

crowd, and smiled as they came toward
her with Harriet and Niall Hawkins.

"We want to thank you both for
all your help getting the farm ready,"
Niall said. "Thanks to you, all our baby
animals have been well cared for while
we've been so busy. The grand opening
is going splendidly. Everyone seems to be
having a great time."

"It's been hard work," Harriet added. "But it's all worth it now that we can see how much the visitors are enjoying our farm."

"Our hard work was worth it, too," Rachel whispered into her best friend's ear.

"And lots of fun as well," Kirsty whispered back.

Niall and Harriet looked happy and relaxed now that everything was going so well. Rachel and Kirsty felt relaxed, too, knowing that Jack Frost would not be causing any more trouble for the Farm Animal Fairies.

"I wonder when we'll have our next adventure with our fairy friends," said Rachel.

"Right now, I want to have an adventure with our new *human* friends," said Kirsty, grinning at Emily and Isabel. "An adventure exploring Greenfields Farm. Let's go!"

RAINBOW
magic™
SPECIAL EDITION

Rachel and Kirsty have found the
Farm Animal Fairies' missing magic animals.
Now it's time for them to help

Michelle
the Winter Wonderland Fairy!

Join their next adventure in this
special sneak peek . . .

The Frosty Ferry

"It was so nice of your mom to invite me on this trip," Rachel Walker said to her best friend, Kirsty Tate. She looked out at the blue waves churning around the ferry and took a deep breath.

"The trip was my mom's prize for winning a painting contest. It was for her favorite travel website," Kirsty explained. Kirsty was proud of her mom. Mrs. Tate's oil painting was beautiful—a stunning close-up of the details of a deep green pine-tree branch, dusted with crystal-white snow. The painting's background was of the serene landscape of snow-covered hills. "I've never been to Snowbound Island before, and this is the weekend of their famous Winter Wonder Festival."

"I've never been to a winter resort, either, but the photos on the website looked almost exactly like your mom's painting," Rachel said.

"Maybe that's why she won!" Kirsty

mused. "You know, my mom said she was looking forward to sleeping in and having breakfast in bed, but I'm just excited to get out in the snow."

"I know. We haven't had any snow at home at all." Even though it was well into December and almost time to celebrate the winter holidays, the weather had been dreary and rainy.

"My dad checked the forecast. They've had tons of snow on the island," Kirsty said.

"I think he was right," Rachel said, pointing.

Kirsty turned to see the sweetest tuft of land. It looked almost like a glacier, rising right out of the crashing waves. From this distance, they could see the ski slopes, treeless paths that curved down the steep mountainside. There was also a large, wooden building with smoke puffing out of the chimney. Kirsty guessed it must be the lodge. As the ferry chugged closer, the water became choppier. Rachel lost her balance, and both girls laughed as they grabbed the railing.

"I can't wait!" Rachel admitted. "I don't know if I want to ski or skate first."

"Or snowshoe or sled," Kirsty added, and then paused. "On second thought, sledding is my first choice. Definitely."

Just then, a door to the boat's cabin opened, and Mr. Tate poked his head outside. "Brrrrr," he said as the wind gusted by. "The captain said the sea is too cold and unruly, so you two need to come inside. There are huge waves and chunks of ice. It's getting dangerous."

RAINBOW magic

Which Magical Fairies Have You Met?

- ❏ The Rainbow Fairies
- ❏ The Weather Fairies
- ❏ The Jewel Fairies
- ❏ The Pet Fairies
- ❏ The Sports Fairies
- ❏ The Ocean Fairies
- ❏ The Princess Fairies
- ❏ The Superstar Fairies
- ❏ The Fashion Fairies
- ❏ The Sugar & Spice Fairies
- ❏ The Earth Fairies
- ❏ The Magical Crafts Fairies
- ❏ The Baby Animal Rescue Fairies
- ❏ The Fairy Tale Fairies
- ❏ The School Day Fairies
- ❏ The Storybook Fairies
- ❏ The Friendship Fairies

■ SCHOLASTIC

HIT entertainment

Find all of your favorite fairy friends at
scholastic.com/rainbowmagic

RMFAIRY17

RAINBOW magic™

SPECIAL EDITION

Which Magical Fairies Have You Met?

- ❑ Joy the Summer Vacation Fairy
- ❑ Holly the Christmas Fairy
- ❑ Kylie the Carnival Fairy
- ❑ Stella the Star Fairy
- ❑ Shannon the Ocean Fairy
- ❑ Trixie the Halloween Fairy
- ❑ Gabriella the Snow Kingdom Fairy
- ❑ Juliet the Valentine Fairy
- ❑ Mia the Bridesmaid Fairy
- ❑ Flora the Dress-Up Fairy
- ❑ Paige the Christmas Play Fairy
- ❑ Emma the Easter Fairy
- ❑ Cara the Camp Fairy
- ❑ Destiny the Rock Star Fairy
- ❑ Belle the Birthday Fairy
- ❑ Olympia the Games Fairy
- ❑ Selena the Sleepover Fairy

- ❑ Cheryl the Christmas Tree Fairy
- ❑ Florence the Friendship Fairy
- ❑ Lindsay the Luck Fairy
- ❑ Brianna the Tooth Fairy
- ❑ Autumn the Falling Leaves Fairy
- ❑ Keira the Movie Star Fairy
- ❑ Addison the April Fool's Day Fairy
- ❑ Bailey the Babysitter Fairy
- ❑ Natalie the Christmas Stocking Fairy
- ❑ Lila and Myla the Twins Fairies
- ❑ Chelsea the Congratulations Fairy
- ❑ Carly the School Fairy
- ❑ Angelica the Angel Fairy
- ❑ Blossom the Flower Girl Fairy
- ❑ Skyler the Fireworks Fairy
- ❑ Giselle the Christmas Ballet Fairy
- ❑ Alicia the Snow Queen Fairy

■ SCHOLASTIC

Find all of your favorite fairy friends at
scholastic.com/rainbowmagic

3 stories in each one!

HiT entertainment

RMSPECIAL20